Thomas Wharton

Hildegard Sings

Farrar, Straus and Giroux

New York

Copyright © 1991 by Thomas Wharton
All rights reserved
Library of Congress catalog card number: 90-55142
Published simultaneously in Canada
by HarperCollins*CanadaLtd*
Designed by Martha Rago
Printed and bound in the United States of America
by Horowitz/Rae Book Manufacturers
First edition, 1991

For my mother

Hildegard Rhineheffer was a singer. She loved singing more than anything in the world, except maybe eating.

During the day, she was a singing waitress in an Italian restaurant, and at night she sang in the chorus of the opera.

Hildegard loved the opera. The music was wonderful, the costumes were fun to wear, and the applause was thrilling. But Hildegard dreamed of being a star.

Hildegard was determined to be ready when her big chance came. She took good care of her voice. She went to her voice lessons, got her beauty sleep, and ate lots of food (just to keep up her strength).

Early one morning, the conductor of the opera, Humphrey Waddlesworth, and the tenor, Bartholomew Bacon, had exciting news. Frau Hoopenholler was ill and Hildegard was going to have to sing the lead that night in a performance for the Queen.

Hildegard was flabbergasted. There was so much to do to get ready. First they all had a big breakfast. Then they went to the music room, so she could try out her voice. She played a few notes on the piano to get her pitches and took a deep breath.

Humphrey and Bartholomew couldn't believe their ears.

"I just don't understand," sputtered Hildegard. "My voice was just fine yesterday. Maybe there's a draft in the room, or maybe I didn't have enough breakfast."

"Now, now," said Bartholomew. "You're just a little nervous. Why don't you relax and try again." Hildegard nodded and took another deep breath.

Hildegard was terrified. Her big chance, and she'd lost her voice. Everyone was going to laugh at her. She would be too embarrassed to go out of her house. She'd have to leave town!

"This will never do," said Humphrey. "We have to think of something to get her voice back!"

They tried *everything*. They had her gargle and sprayed her throat. They gave her hot tea with honey and lemon. They shoveled cough drops into her mouth. They had her take hot bubble baths and put ice on her head.

They gave her mountains of food and a fancy new hat.
They even took her to Madame Zelda, the astrologer,
who counted the bumps on the bottoms of her feet and
gave her some lucky charms.

Nothing seemed to help. Hildegard couldn't sing a note. But, just as they were ready to give up hope, Bartholomew had an idea.

He whispered to Humphrey, "Bring Hildegard to the
opera house tonight. Tell her that I will send her something backstage that I'm sure will bring her voice back."

So Humphrey took her to the opera house and told her to put on her makeup and costume and wait back-stage for Bartholomew and his cure.

She was *very* nervous. Why did she ever want to be an opera singer? What had happened to her voice? What if the audience threw rotten tomatoes at her? What was she going to do?

The opera house began to fill. The musicians in the orchestra took their places. When the Queen arrived, everyone stood and greeted her with applause. Then the conductor stepped forward and the lights went down.

Hildegard heard the applause fade, and the orchestra
began to play. There was a knock at the door.

"It's time for your entrance, Miss Rhineheffer," said the
stage manager.

She left her dressing room and slowly made her way through the dark set. The stagehands were frantically finishing the adjustments to the scenery and lights.

"Places, everyone," called the stage manager, and they all hurried off the stage. Hildegard stood alone behind the curtain.

Her heart was pounding, and her knees began to
wobble. Where on earth was Bartholomew!

"Curtain up," someone shouted.

The lights on the stage started getting brighter. The
sound of the orchestra swelled, and the curtain began
to rise.

Suddenly Bartholomew burst through the stage door,
carrying a small box. He tossed the box to Hildegard.
"Quick, open the box!" he shouted.

She grabbed the box and tore it open. A mouse
popped out, ran up her sleeve and down her dress. She
gasped, spun around, and let out a tremendous . . .

aaaaaaaaaaaaaaaaaaaaaaaaa!

From that moment on, she sang better than she ever had before, and when the opera was over, there was an explosion of cheers and applause.

Hildegard was a star.